I0567564

STORIES ON JOHN STREET

LILLY PEREZ CORTEZ

Dedicated to all the girls and boys with big dreams;

Isabella Cortez and Michael Cortez

Let's dream together

Copyright @ 2021 by Lilly Perez Cortez. All rights reserved.

The Dragonfly Run

The sun peeks through the curtains as I lay deep in a world of magic, Mama comes pushing open the curtains in her assertive voice, "*Ya, mucho de dormir, te va ser daño el sol.*" Staggering out of bed, I finally fumble over to the kitchen table where the smell of vanilla penetrates my nose. I always love Mama's Cream of Wheat that tasted like vanilla cake, and the stack of buttery toast that always accompanied my yummy bowl. The sunlight glowing through the screen door and the sounds of birds chirping catch my interest. I begin to perk up and think of all the things Isabella and I will do today. No sooner as I finish my breakfast, I'm out the door. I hear mama's voice, "¡ *Y no andas entrando y saliendo. Le voy poner el candado a la puerta!*" reminding me that I won't be allowed to go in and out of the house.

It's ok. I have the water hose outside, and when I'm hungry, I simply can eat the fruit that she has growing out in the back. So it's safe to say that I'm well equipped to stay out all day. Plus, Isabella's house is open when no

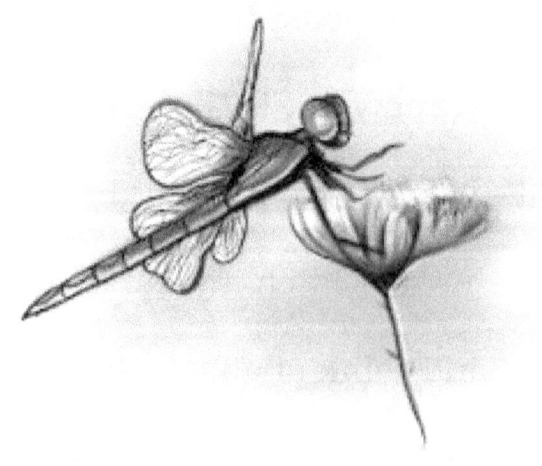

one is around, and that seemed like every

day. We never really need to stay indoors. There is just so much to do.

Once outside, I easily get distracted by the countless dragonflies swooping over me and around me. Why I always thought that I could catch one, beats me, but I always tried anyways. They tease me and come close then jet away. Maybe I could trick them and walk over to the rose bush waiting for it to land. One or two would play along, or maybe they were showing off their brilliant colors and their big bulgy eyes. Many times, I would just stop and admire them. What intriguing insects God made! You know, Mama always said that God made all the creatures, but for what purpose did He make the dragonfly? Maybe just for me to love and play with.

Finally, I remember Isabella, and so I walk over to the front of the yard, carefully analyzing which way I should go to get to her house. Will I be able to run through Luz's yard without her catching me? But if she sees me, she will definitely yell from the top of her lungs, "Don't be going through my yard. Get off my grass!"

Then Mama will get mad at me for having to hear Luz's voice. They never got along. Mama said Luz was jealous and was mean to Daddy, who was her nephew. Mama would grumble, "*Esa mujer nunca está contenta. Es bien mala; no se meten con ella.*"

Well, I knew she didn't like us, but I had no idea why. I think she just doesn't like dirty, sweaty, little girls around her house.

Hmm... This time, I decide to get to Isabella's house by walking on the edge of the street while looking out for stray dogs that sometimes pop out from underneath parked cars. The coast is clear. I then head down the street to the other side of Luz's yard. I fly like a dragonfly. As I come up to the gate, I'm greeted by Lalo and Chato. They come out of the little doggie door from the porch and bounce up and down wagging their little stump of a tail. They are the happiest miniature Boston Terriers. I carefully open the gate door, because I don't want to let them out and escape. They are heavy little things as I feel them bouncing off my legs. At last, I make it to the porch door, and already, Isabella is walking out onto the porch.

"Hey Isabella!" Excitedly greeting her as if I have not seen her for ages. We are best cousins and playmates. Plus, we are the youngest of all the cousins that live in the Smith Edition. So, we are well protected and fear very little—except the wrath of making our older siblings mad. However, there's no need to be afraid from anyone else in the hood. Free like dragonflies, we had friends all around us, and being the youngest also helps you get adopted by the older kids from the neighborhood. It is a happy time and a loving place to grow up.

The Banana Seat Ride

"What? Aww, Man! I want to ride it. Please, pretty please."

Santiago was the coolest. My brother could fix anything, and he is super smart. No one can beat him. I'm going to be just like him. I don't know where he finds these things, but he's the best. He can make model cars, fix our skateboards, and we never have to worry about our bikes. If the chain falls off, we go to

Santiago. If the brake on our bikes don't work, we go to Santiago. If the seat of our bike falls off, you guessed it. We go to Santiago. He always brings home the best.

It was the perfect summer day. Dolores, Maria, Isabella, Pati and of course I were all outside having fun. I like being around all the older girls. They can be loud and crazy. Boy crazy that is. Isabella and I have fun laughing at them. We listen to their stories and who they are going to marry and how many kids they are going to have. They all share the perfect wedding day story about the boy that they have kissed. Yuck, Isabella and I would squirm every time they said they kissed a boy.

According to Maria, she was the master at kissing boys. I never saw her with a boy. Then again, maybe she was hiding when she was kissing them. Hmm... On the other hand, we didn't have a lot of hiding places either. Oh well, it was time to get moving, and there goes Dolores, my older sister, pulling out one of the many cool bikes Santiago found for us.

This one was the best bike. Long handlebars with plastic grip handles, and it wasn't too big like the ten-speed bike in the garage. It was medium size, but the best part was the seat. I love that big, long red seat made to fit two of us because I didn't always get a chance to ride it by myself. Nonetheless, there was always room for me on the seat or a place on the spokes to get a ride. Boy, we could fit up to three people on that bike and sometimes even four. One of the boys would have been pedaling the bike for four of us because we girls could only manage three. The weight was too heavy, and we would all fall over.

Today, we have been giving each other rides up and down the street. Dolores and her skinny legs were quickly speeding back and forth then dropping off the passenger for the next person. At one point she and Pati, her best friend who was just as boy crazy as Dolores, thought they were so cool racing back and forth on the bike with the banana seat. Dolores raced right past us as we shouted, "My turn, my turn!" No luck, Dolores was going too fast, and all we could hear were the giggles coming from Pati as she got a free ride. We screamed louder as they rode by and cheered them on. I guess Dolores forgot how much Pati weighed, and with the lightning-fast speed, those skinny legs just couldn't break. Crossing the street...Bam! Right into a car.

All we could see was Dolores and Pati bouncing off that big red seat and falling over. Lucky for them, the car was just cruising slowly. Man! We saw that man jump out of his car to check on them, but I guess Dolores and

Pati were more scared that Mom and Dad were going to see them. They jumped up and picked up the banana seat bike and quickly started walking back to the driveway. At first, we were scared, but when we saw them almost running back with that bike, we all burst out laughing. The coast was clear; no one saw what happened, and we were all good. Dolores put the bike down. She was done for the day. Yesss! Finally, my turn to ride.

"Please, can I ride it?" I shouted. "Yeah. I'm not riding that thing," as if it was the bikes fault for Dolores crashing. I wrapped my legs over that bike and stood on the peddles ready to push off when I casually sat back on the banana seat. "Ay!" The banana seat popped up and I go rolling back onto the street. Aw man! Where was Santiago?

The Sanchez Kids

Friday night and here come *los compadres*. Their bright green van parks in front of the driveway and they hop out greeting us loudly and enthusiastically. They are a happy couple and always driving everywhere. It seemed like they were the Google Maps of the 80's, and the countless stories of adventures they had made all of us want to sit around the table to listen to them. I loved the boxes of textiles and gifts they would bring which meant more fashion creations for me to sew on mama's sewing machine.

Put on the coffee and bring out the conchas. It was social night!

I know I have heard the stories before but being part of the group comforted me. I belonged there and besides, I loved sitting right next to Mama.

Of course, I had to be on the side of the women until Daddy called out for something. Then I would shrug my shoulders when the compadre would say, "Hey Chief, esta gordita se parece todo a ti." I really didn't like it when they would call me "la gordita," but Daddy's big hug and his proud reply, "That's my baby right there," made it ok. Then I was shushed back over to the women's side of the table right next to Mama. We laughed hard at every story told as if it was the first time we heard it. It probably was the hundredth time, but that never mattered. We are having a great time with the *compadres*. However, I always wondered where the kids were because I could use a playmate at this time.

And speaking of kids, the Sanchez's had a bunch. Thirteen to be exact! Thirteen kids that all fit in one house next to the chemical plant. I played with Monica. She was closer to my age, but boy, when we played tag with the others, it would get loud and crazy. They were good kids just a bit wild.

Like one time, I remember Jesus getting mad at us for running away and hiding for too long. When we came back out, he threw a glass bottle at us. What a bad aim he had! Oh boy! When Monica ran in to tell on him, there was total silence. She came back out and shouted, "Jesus, Dad wants you inside!"

He was already crying before he even entered the house. Back then, belts and paddles were our forms of corrections. We didn't know about parents sitting down and having a conversation about what not to do and why. It was just the way of life, and our parents didn't have time for a lengthy explanation. A quick spanking and move on.

We'd better think before we do it or our butts would be whipped. Maybe that's why I never saw the kids with the *compadres* at our house. I only played with them when we would go to their house. I always saw them running and shouting at each other in their yard, popping wheelies and riding through the ditches on their bikes. The older ones playing the latest hits on the boom box. We were somewhat carefree as long as no one told the parents.

Then one day, I told my fourth-grade teacher, Ms. Anderson, about them. Only I changed things a bit, just to help me out for a while. By fourth grade, I began to test the waters, or more like drown in the waters. So, I took on being a Sanchez. At that time, I hated having to come home and recite my multiplication and work on division. It was boring and took too long. The days were shorter, and I had less time to go outside and play with Isabella. But the Sanchez family issues would solve that problem.

You see, after so many years of having babies and leaving them to be cared for by the oldest daughter, Sandra, it began to take its toll on her. She wanted her independence and her own teenage life to learn and explore. Well, she decided she had enough. Late one night, there was knocking at our front door. It was the *Compadre* and worried as could be. He explained how Sandra ran away from home, and they couldn't find her.

What? I couldn't believe it. I knew the kids were a bit wild, but these stories were finally getting juicy. After all, it was nightfall. Where would she go? Is she safe? Man! I would be scared. Dad took off with the *Compadre,* and we all stayed up a bit to talk about where she could have gone, and how surprised we were. Really? Anyone would run away after taking care of so many kids and not going out with friends once in a while. Poor Sandra. Finally, Mom insisted we go back to bed since we had school tomorrow.

Wait! What? I forgot I hadn't done my homework for tomorrow. Yikes! I'm going to have to meet with Ms. Anderson about why I don't have my homework. What's going to happen when she tells dad? Oh, what a mess! Hey, wait! I thought of the perfect excuse. Sandra ran away. Yeah, Ms. Anderson won't know. Why, Sandra could be my sister for all she knows. After all, we were close to the *compadres*, and they were considered family. Problem solved.

A week passed, and the drama from the Sanchez's was working just fine. I was given several passes on homework. Thank goodness they found Sandra and promised to listen to her and not leave so much responsibility on her. What was even better was no school tomorrow due to parent conferences. Dad made sure to check the calendar and his written notes for when he had to visit the schools. Dad always took care of parent teacher conference days because Mom didn't speak English and didn't think that she would understand. Now, why didn't I see where this was going? I even went with Dad to show him where my room was.

I thought I was just too cool. Anyway, Ms. Anderson likes me, and she was nice. But wait, Parent/Teacher Conference Day was about showing Dad my progress and grades, not just about the teacher liking me. Dad's face looked confused when Ms. Anderson asked me to step out of the room for a moment. Uh oh. What was she going to tell him? Surely, she won't mention the deal about Sandra. That would be too hurtful and embarrassing for Dad if that was his real daughter. The door opened, and Dad walked out with that frown he would make with his little lips that you could hardly see under his thick mustache. Not a word spoken on the way home. At that point, I knew I was going get it.

As we walked in, Dad tells Mom how I told Ms. Anderson a whole lie that my sister ran away. "¡Ay! Luna." That was all I remember hearing from Mom while Dad rearranged the living room. I was surprised to not see the *correa* come out, nor did I see it come out again. I think Dad and Mom learned something from the Sanchez's too. Dad placed a desk facing a wall and told me to start writing my multiplications on a large stack of index cards. I was grounded and wouldn't see Isabella for a whole month. The tears ran down my cheek, and I began to learn 1 X 1=1.

The Parade Shout Out

Back at Isabella's house with Lalo and Chato, the cutest dogs ever, I wait for Isabella to come out. "Hey girl, ready?"

The best part about living in a small neighborhood and being Latina was knowing practically everyone because most of your relatives live there. Even if they are not blood relatives, you still call them family. Why I even have a black blood-sister. Yolanda who would come yelling down the street, "Hey pops, where's everybody?" She always gave out the best hugs and had the nicest voice. I was her little sister, and we treated each other with love and care. The family always included Yolanda to the movies, to Pizza Inn, play time at the house, and volleyball in the streets.

You see, the Chicanos and the Blacks made up most of Smith Edition along with the new immigrants. The Blacks and the Chicanos were tied together by the English language. Since it was not cool to speak Spanish in school, we felt a closer tie to the Blacks, and along with Soul Train and the boom box playing disco, it was a lot of fun hanging out. To us kids, we were just a bunch of kids with good ideas and close friendships. We could relate to one another.

Another thing, volleyball always brought us together. Here comes Dolores with the volleyball and Pati running out onto the street. The sound of the ball bouncing off the asphalt street seemed to call attention, or maybe it was Dolores and Pati calling out "Car!" Nevertheless, we always end up with a crowd ready to serve the ball. No net was needed; the line from the different color asphalt patch served as the division of the court. Once we became tired of playing ball, Isabella and I would go walking around the block or venture to the warehouses at the end of the neighborhood.

Three houses of pure Perez's lined John Street, and the *compadres* at the corner who always watched the comings and goings of everyone. When we turn the corner, we would see Suzie and the *compadres* waving letting us know that we are among family. I always felt like I was in a parade waving to all the *compadres*, family members, and all the childhood friends who all went to the same schools. There is always someone looking out for the other. Even when you're in the car, it was like the royal family driving down the street. Thank goodness Dad was into real-estate and bought up the large lots. Where else would we have our birthday parties to include all our family and friends?

The parties were the best, and the parade of people would end up in our backyard. They started at three in the afternoon and would run through the night. Sometimes we had a real *conjunto* come out and play while the brisket slowly cooked in the pit. I never understood why Dad always said we weren't rich, and it was hell to be poor. I never felt poor except when we would leave Smith Edition to see the popular neighborhoods of town. It was a car trip that we never got out. Anyway, that was only once a year. The rest of my time was spent in the loving arms of Smith Edition.

Stories on John Street

Sunday Morning Battle

Sunday mornings were sacred rituals

that tortured me every week. Mom was always

calling and threatening to spank us if we didn't

hurry up and get dressed for church. I was too

tired, and I wasn't looking forward to seeing Mr. Cantu. He was the church usher who thought he owned the church. Besides, I never saw him when we were there on Saturday polishing the pews and sweeping the floors. Plus, I couldn't stand him telling us kids to be quiet while he and the other ushers stood around talking. Momma always gave me a nudge on my side when I would turn my head to let him know that I could hear him.

I didn't like only the early morning rise, but also the long kneeling moments, and especially the restraint of me having to stay quiet, or else God would punish us. Mom always said God is watching, and we are in His house. The elder women always made sure to read us the stories of God punishing people for eating forbidden fruits and flooding the world because people didn't follow God's rules. For me, going to church was seeing everyone and having breakfast while we socialize. After that, it was Sunday class time and boring all over again. More scary stories were told of God punishing different people. Instead, I wanted to be outside running around the trees and watching everyone. Mom always had us in some kind of church class even during the week.

Don't get me wrong. We had a lot of recreational events, and those were the best with all the float decorations for *el Día de la Virgen de Guadalupe*, Christmas *posadas*, bazaars, even Halloween trick-or-treat parties and so much more. Great friendships were made, and fun memories will forever run through my mind. However, during rest of the year, we endured the Legion of Mary meetings,

Sunday classes, and long mass times sitting quietly.

On the other hand, Mama never left her *curandera* spiritual rituals. The weekly blessing of the house, and the visits to the *yerberias* to buy herbs, and spiritual artifacts to cure us and bless us all at the same time were taken seriously. Her spiritual eggs and deer eyes did wonders for us. The little flowers secretly placed on my shirt that would protect me at school and give me confidence to make hard choices was my super-power. I love the scents from the burning coals and *yerbas* that Mama would light while blessing the house. I liked that I was included and got to take part in either jumping over the coals or spreading the holy blessings with holy water. Faith is a big thing in my family.

We believed alright in a higher power, but ironically, it didn't always keep us out of trouble. Such as the time when Rosalinda threw a fit in the church during our Legion of Mary prayer session. I guess she wanted to see if the Good Lord would strike her down like the elders had always threatened. You could see the anger boiling up in her, and no one knew why she was so troubled. Her mom tried desperately to quiet her down, but Rosalinda just wasn't having it. My eyes were fixed on her because I have never seen God send down a punishment and boy, would that be a story!

Rosalinda couldn't hold it in any longer. She stood up and shouted "Shut up!" along with a line of curse words aimed at everyone including the Virgin Mary. I felt my heart pounding, and a chill came over me. Looking up for the bolt of lightning to come crashing down on Rosalinda, I feared that it might have a cascading effect and catch the church on fire. All I could see was her mom and older sister grabbing her by each arm and taking her out of the church. There was no bolt of lightning not even a tiny flash.

My mind began to race. How can you curse out the Virgin Mary and not get punished by God? In the neighborhood, if you talked bad about anyone's mama, you were sure to end up in a fight or get smacked. So...what happened to the ultimate punishment from God in His

house that would get us to settle down?

Hmmm... maybe the elders didn't quite have it

right.

Time to write your own. . .

www.ingramcontent.com/pod-product-compliance
Lightning Source LLC
Chambersburg PA
CBHW070355130626
46556CB00007B/3181